MARVEL

BLACK PANTHER

MARVEL
marvelkids.com

© 2018 MARVEL

Illustrations by Steve Kurth

Cover design by Elaine Lopez-Levine. Cover illustration by Steve Kurth.

Little, Brown and Company
Hachette Book Group
1290 Avenue of the Americas, New York, NY 10104
Visit us at LBYR.com
marvelkids.com

First Edition: January 2018

Little, Brown and Company is a division of Hachette Book Group, Inc.
The Little, Brown name and logo are trademarks of Hachette Book Group, Inc.

The publisher is not responsible for websites (or their content) that are not owned by the publisher.

Library of Congress Control Number 2017954820

ISBNs: 978-0-316-41381-7 (pbk.), 978-0-316-41382-4 (ebook), 978-0-316-41384-8 (ebook), 978-0-316-41380-0 (ebook)

Printed in the United States of America

CW

10 9 8 7 6 5 4 3

MARVEL
BLACK PANTHER

ON THE PROWL!

Adapted by R. R. Busse
Illustrations by Steve Kurth
Produced by Kevin Feige, p.g.a.
Directed by Ryan Coogler
Written by Ryan Coogler & Joe Robert Cole

LITTLE, BROWN AND COMPANY
New York   Boston

T'Challa is the future king of Wakanda, a technologically advanced and highly secretive African country. He is a leader of his people, but also their protector—as the Black Panther. He has a suit made of impervious vibranium and has a vast array of technology at his disposal as well as incredible speed and strength.

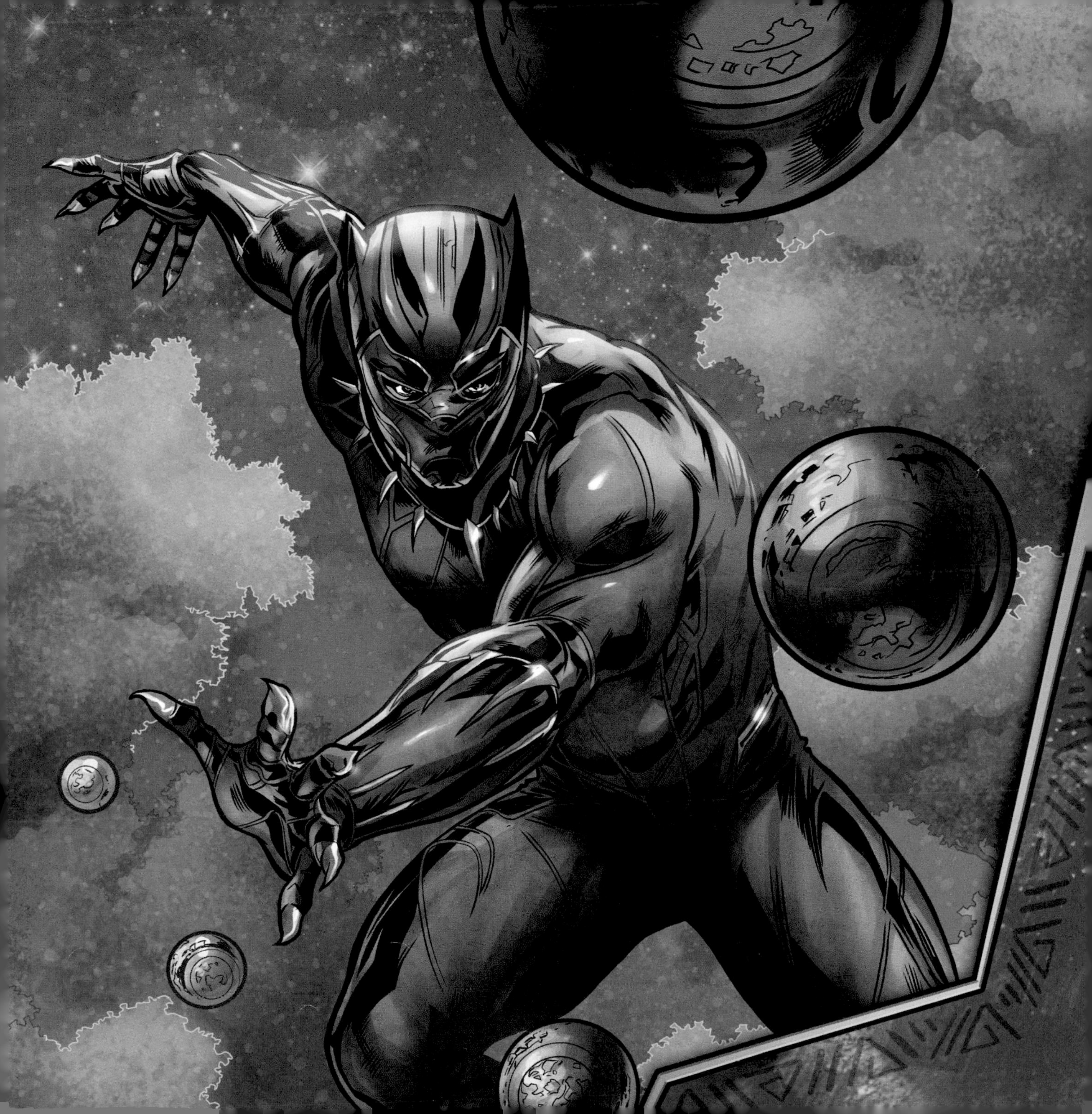

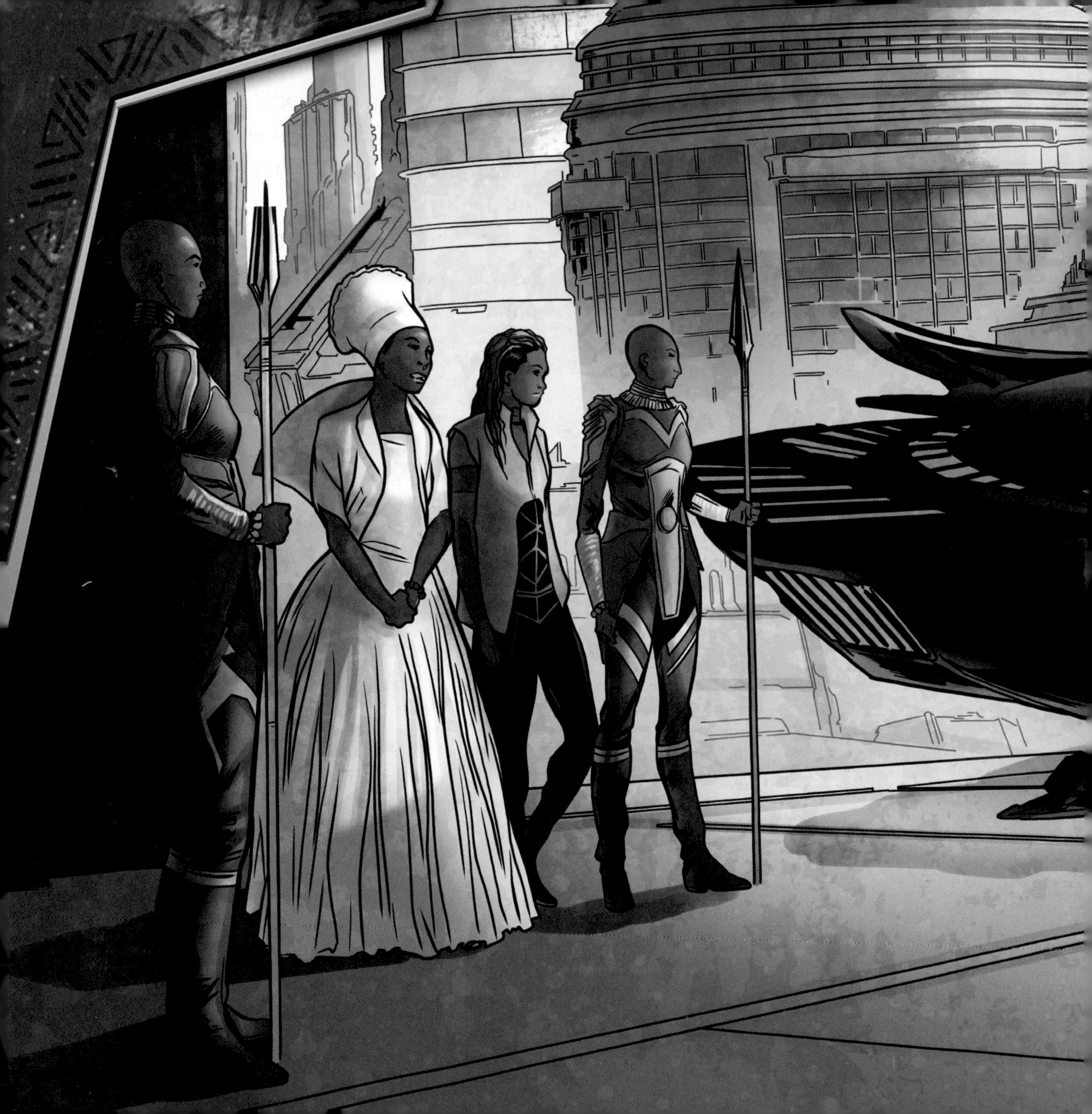

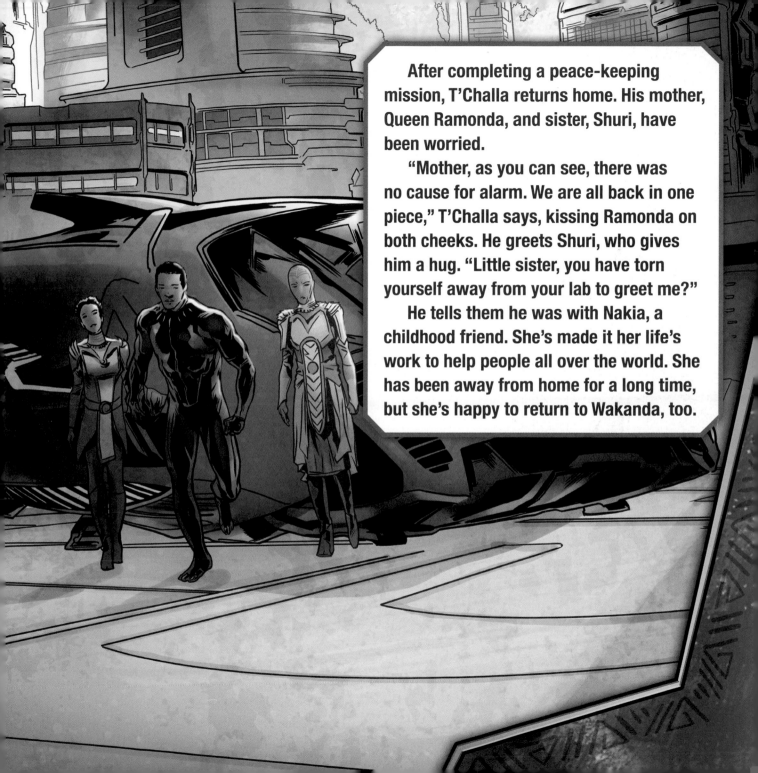

After completing a peace-keeping mission, T'Challa returns home. His mother, Queen Ramonda, and sister, Shuri, have been worried.

"Mother, as you can see, there was no cause for alarm. We are all back in one piece," T'Challa says, kissing Ramonda on both cheeks. He greets Shuri, who gives him a hug. "Little sister, you have torn yourself away from your lab to greet me?"

He tells them he was with Nakia, a childhood friend. She's made it her life's work to help people all over the world. She has been away from home for a long time, but she's happy to return to Wakanda, too.

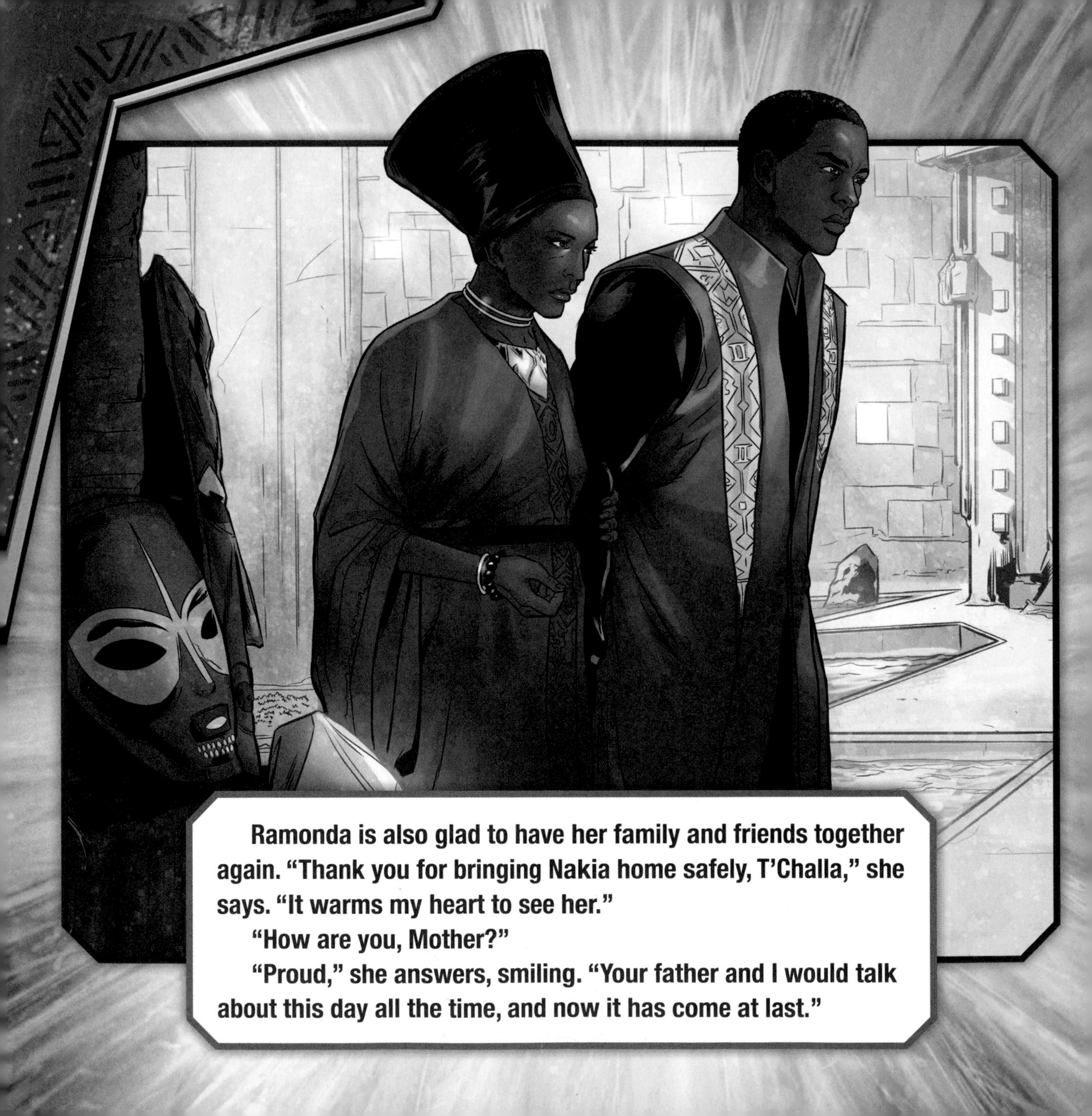

Ramonda is also glad to have her family and friends together again. “Thank you for bringing Nakia home safely, T’Challa,” she says. “It warms my heart to see her.”

“How are you, Mother?”

“Proud,” she answers, smiling. “Your father and I would talk about this day all the time, and now it has come at last.”

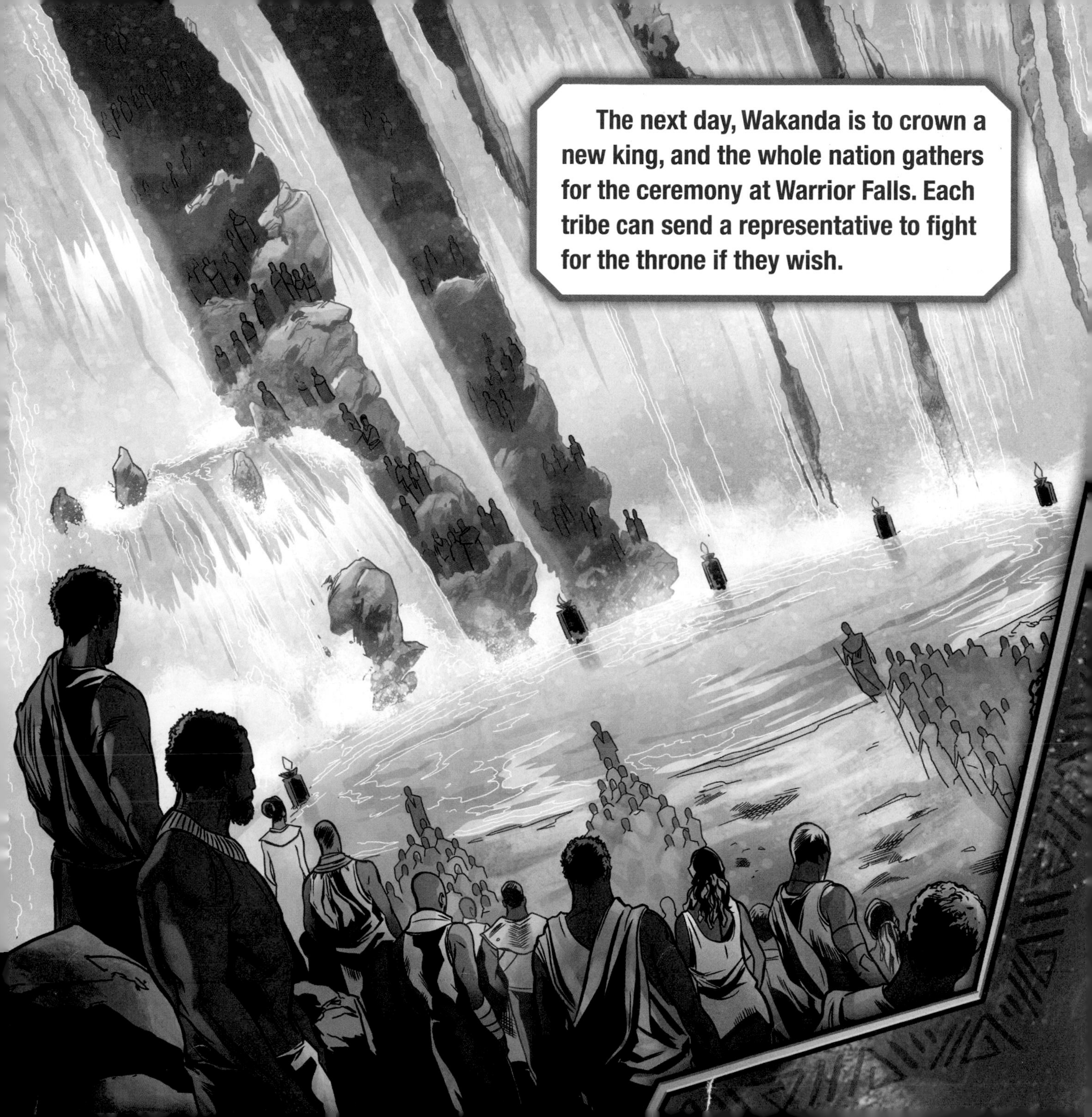
The next day, Wakanda is to crown a new king, and the whole nation gathers for the ceremony at Warrior Falls. Each tribe can send a representative to fight for the throne if they wish.

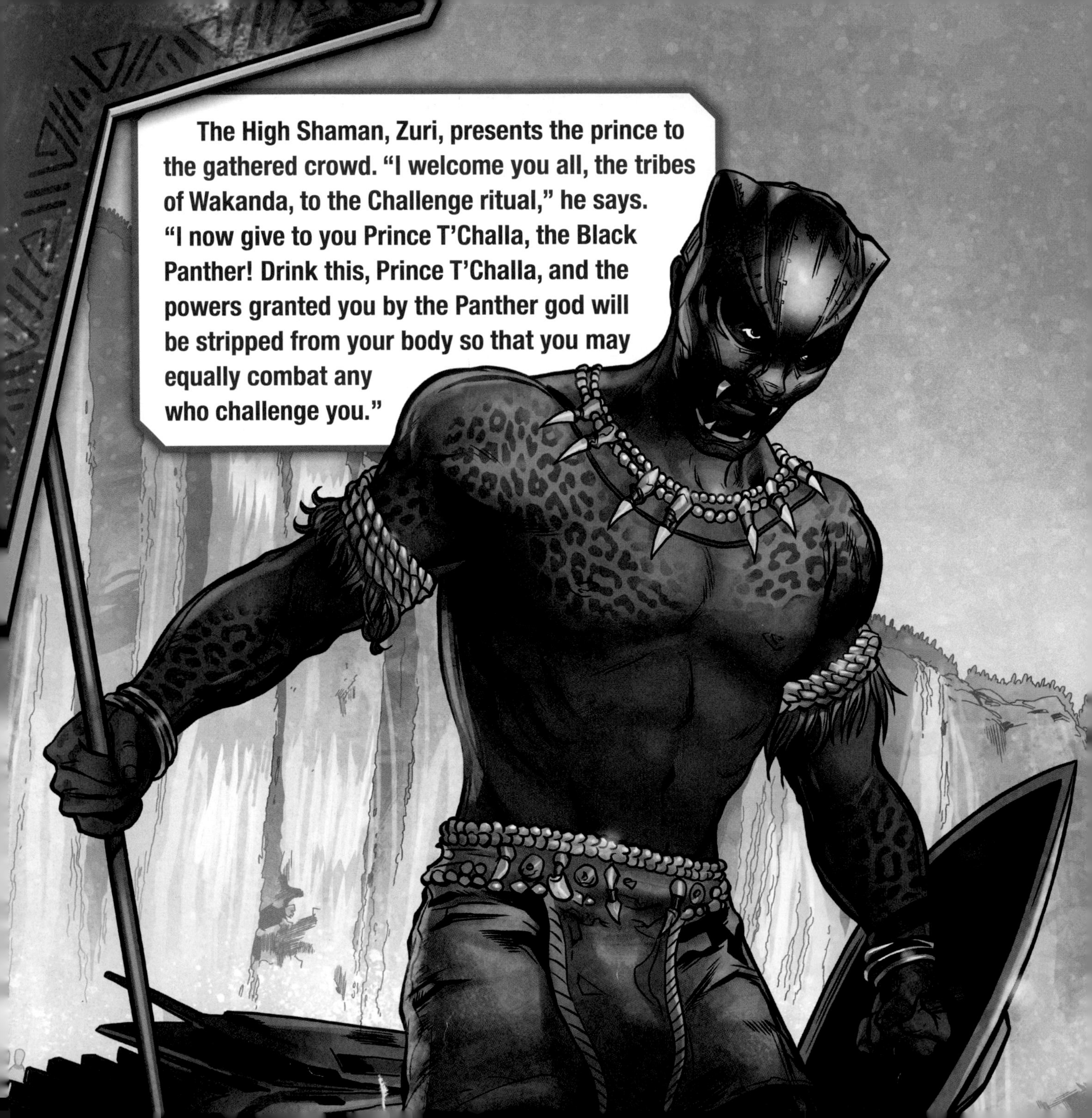

The High Shaman, Zuri, presents the prince to the gathered crowd. “I welcome you all, the tribes of Wakanda, to the Challenge ritual,” he says. “I now give to you Prince T’Challa, the Black Panther! Drink this, Prince T’Challa, and the powers granted you by the Panther god will be stripped from your body so that you may equally combat any who challenge you.”

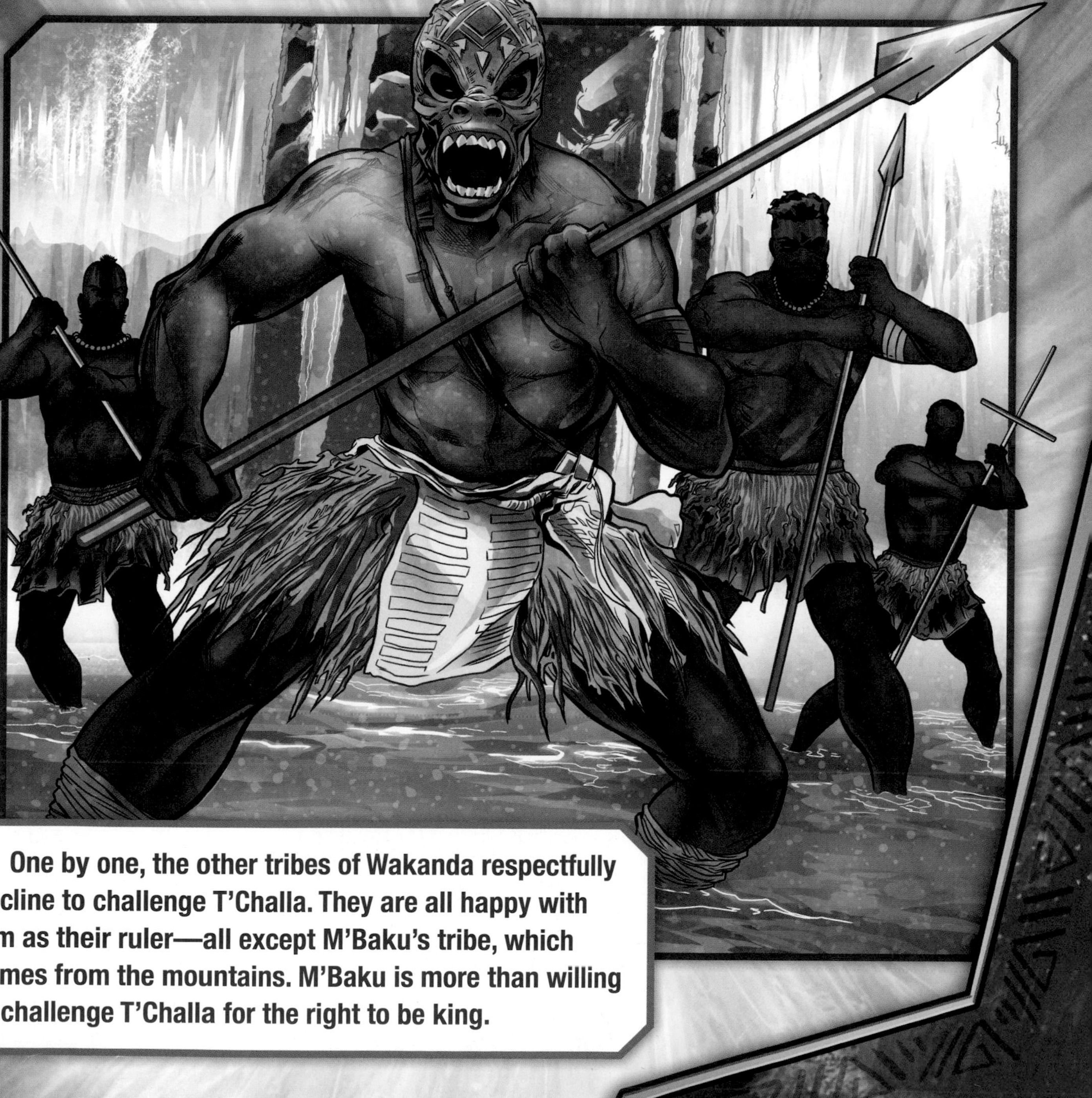

One by one, the other tribes of Wakanda respectfully decline to challenge T'Challa. They are all happy with him as their ruler—all except M'Baku's tribe, which comes from the mountains. M'Baku is more than willing to challenge T'Challa for the right to be king.

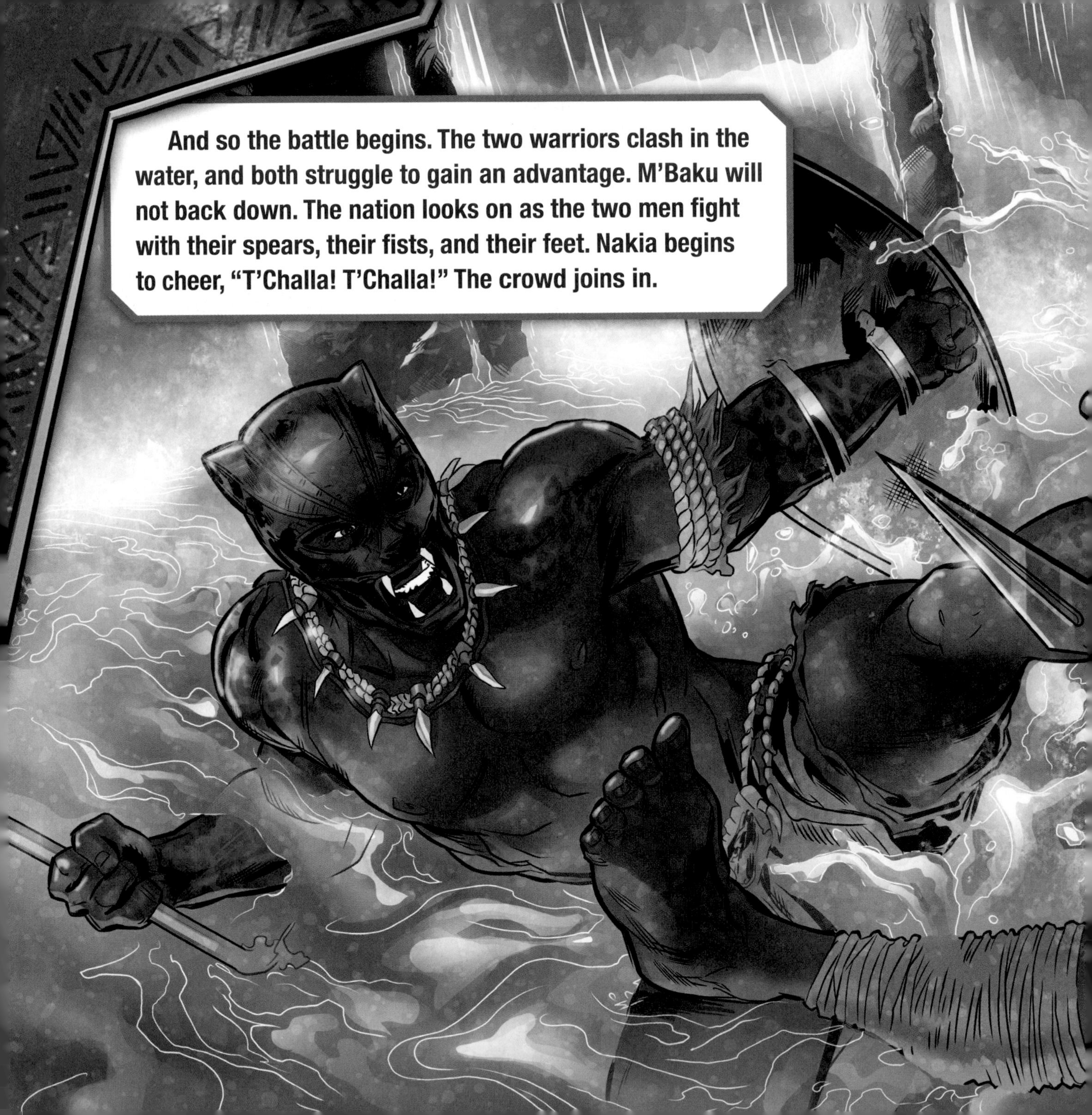

And so the battle begins. The two warriors clash in the water, and both struggle to gain an advantage. M'Baku will not back down. The nation looks on as the two men fight with their spears, their fists, and their feet. Nakia begins to cheer, "T'Challa! T'Challa!" The crowd joins in.

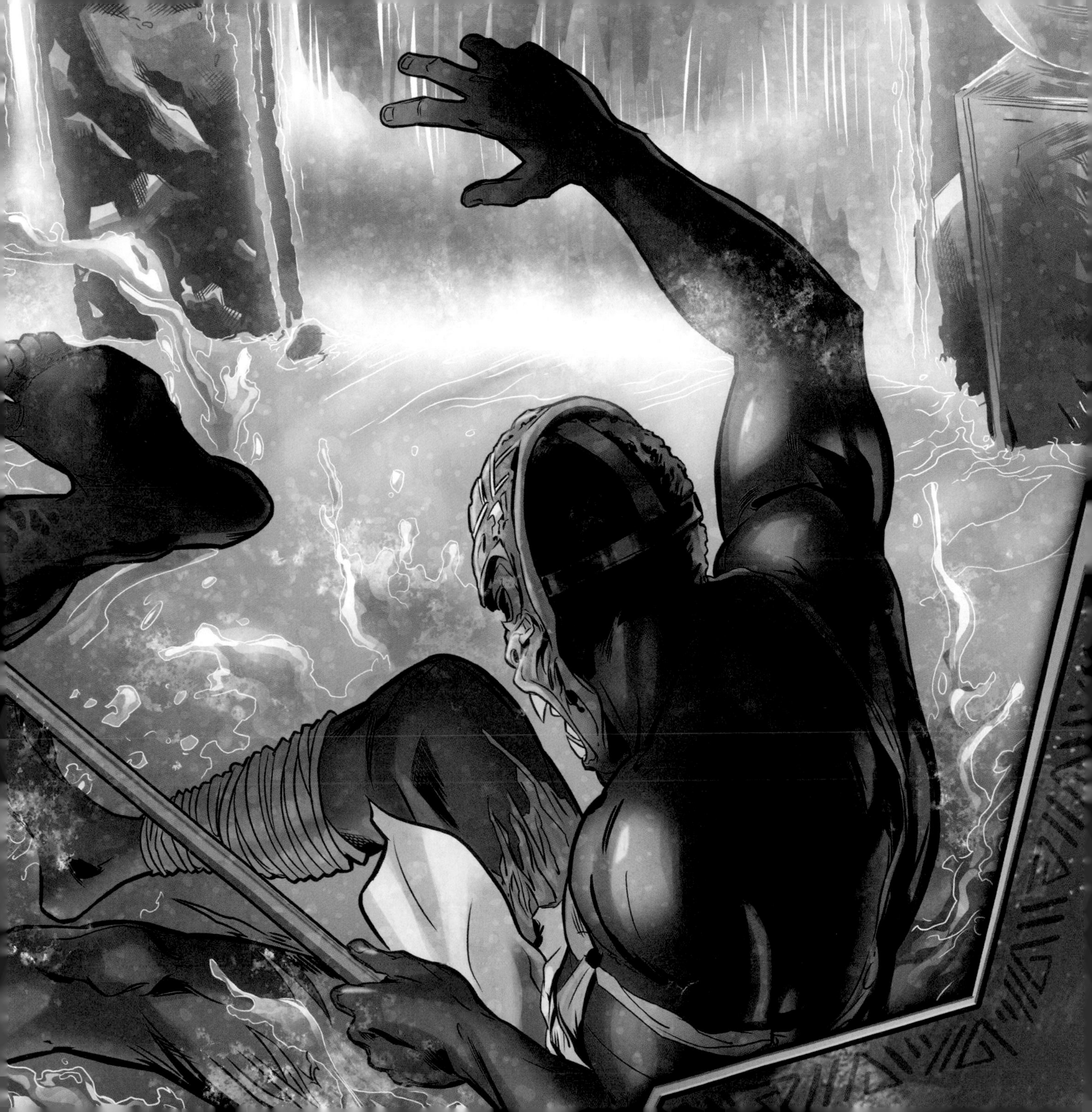

Encouraged by the spirit of his people, T'Challa finally gains the upper hand.

"Yield!" T'Challa yells. "Please. For your tribesmen."

M'Baku finally yields. The battle is over, and the ceremony is complete. T'Challa is the new king of Wakanda.

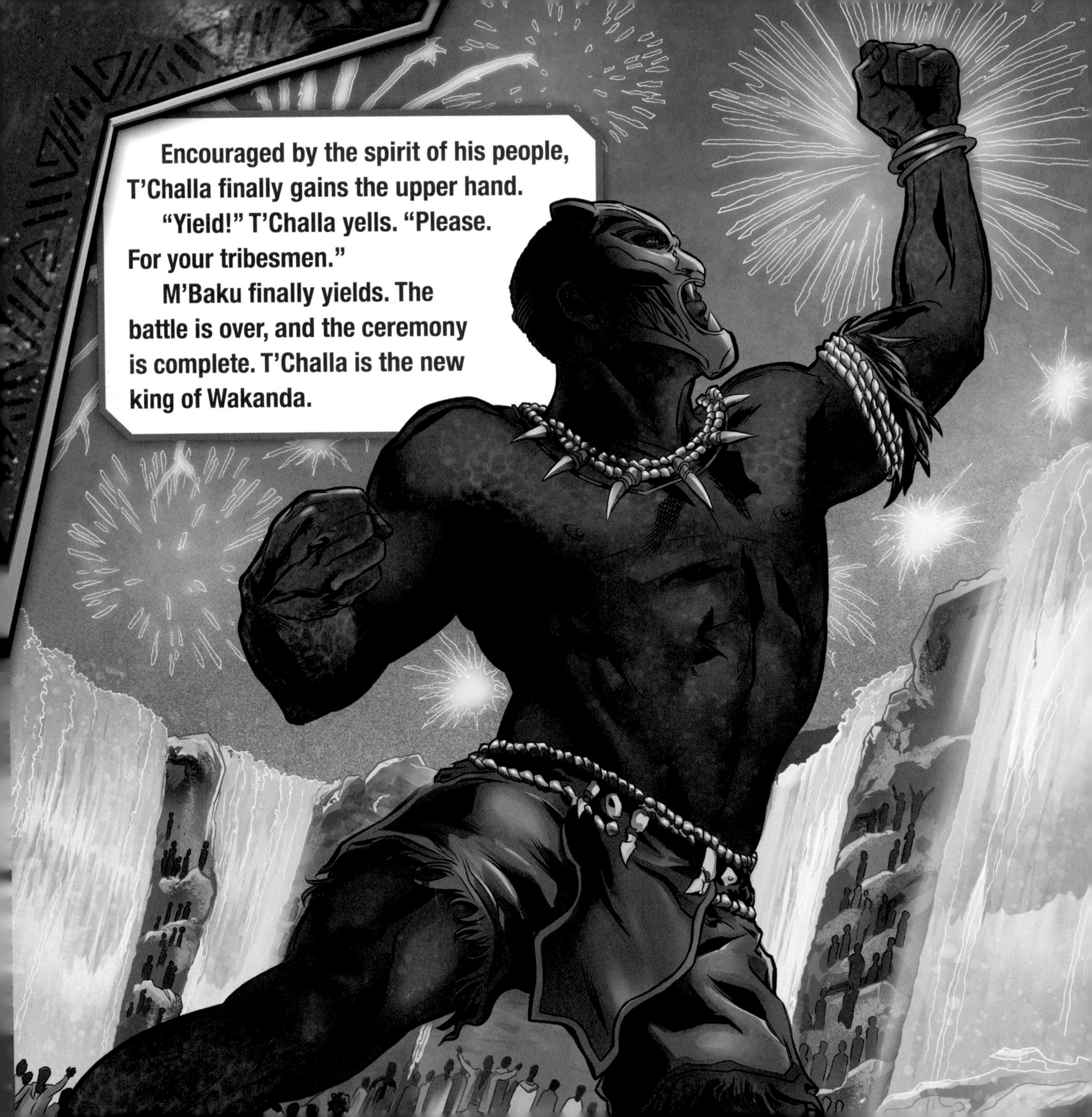

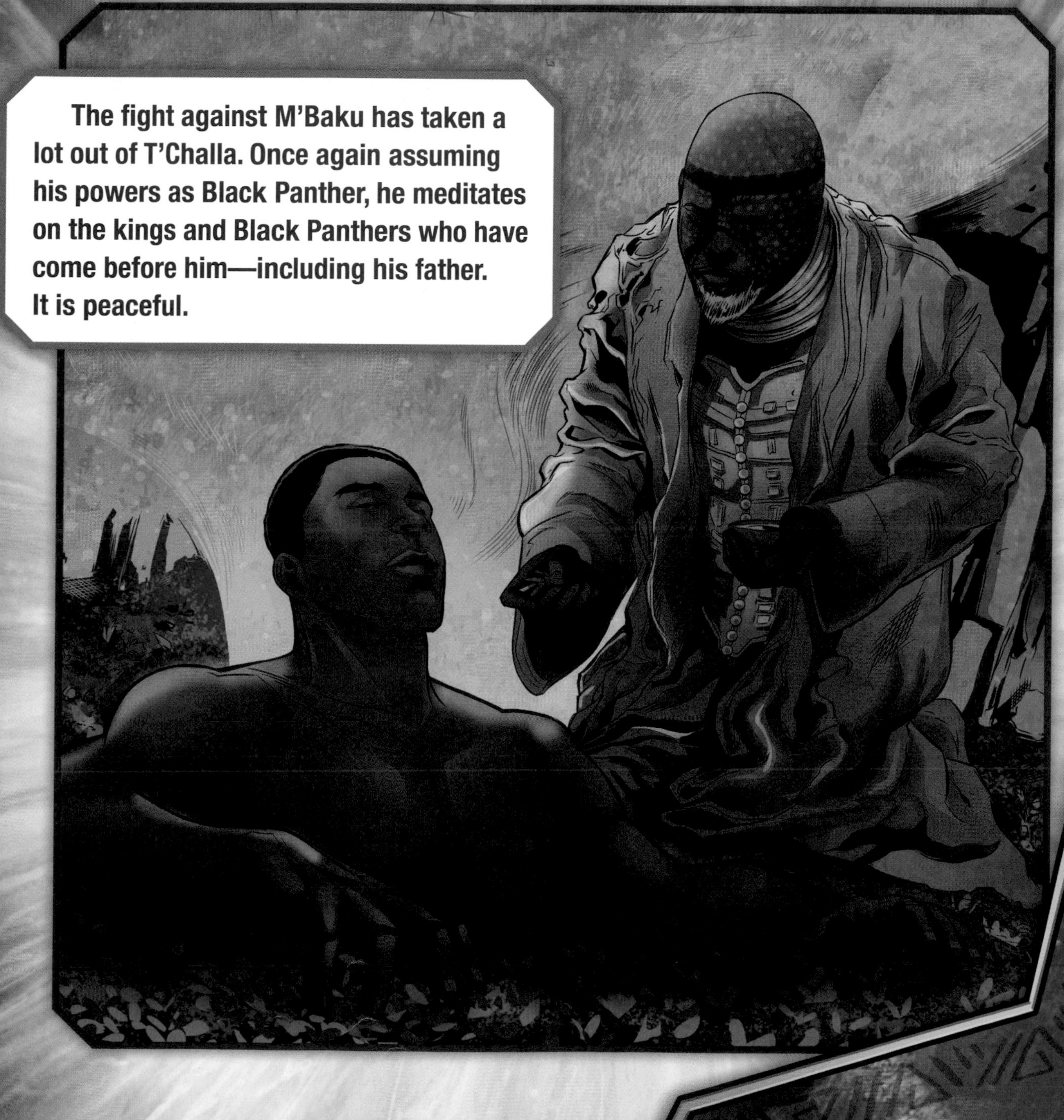
The fight against M'Baku has taken a lot out of T'Challa. Once again assuming his powers as Black Panther, he meditates on the kings and Black Panthers who have come before him—including his father. It is peaceful.

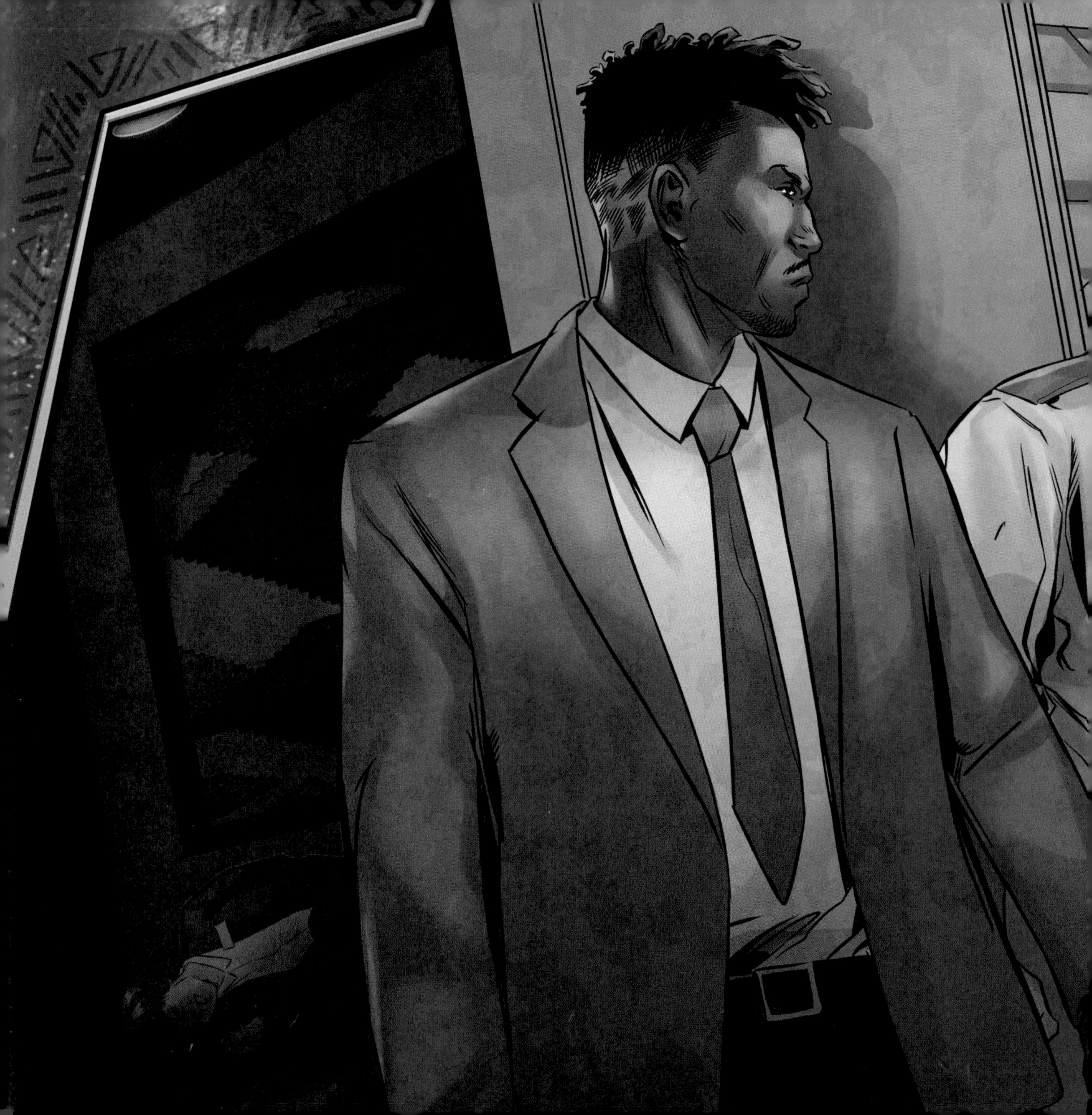

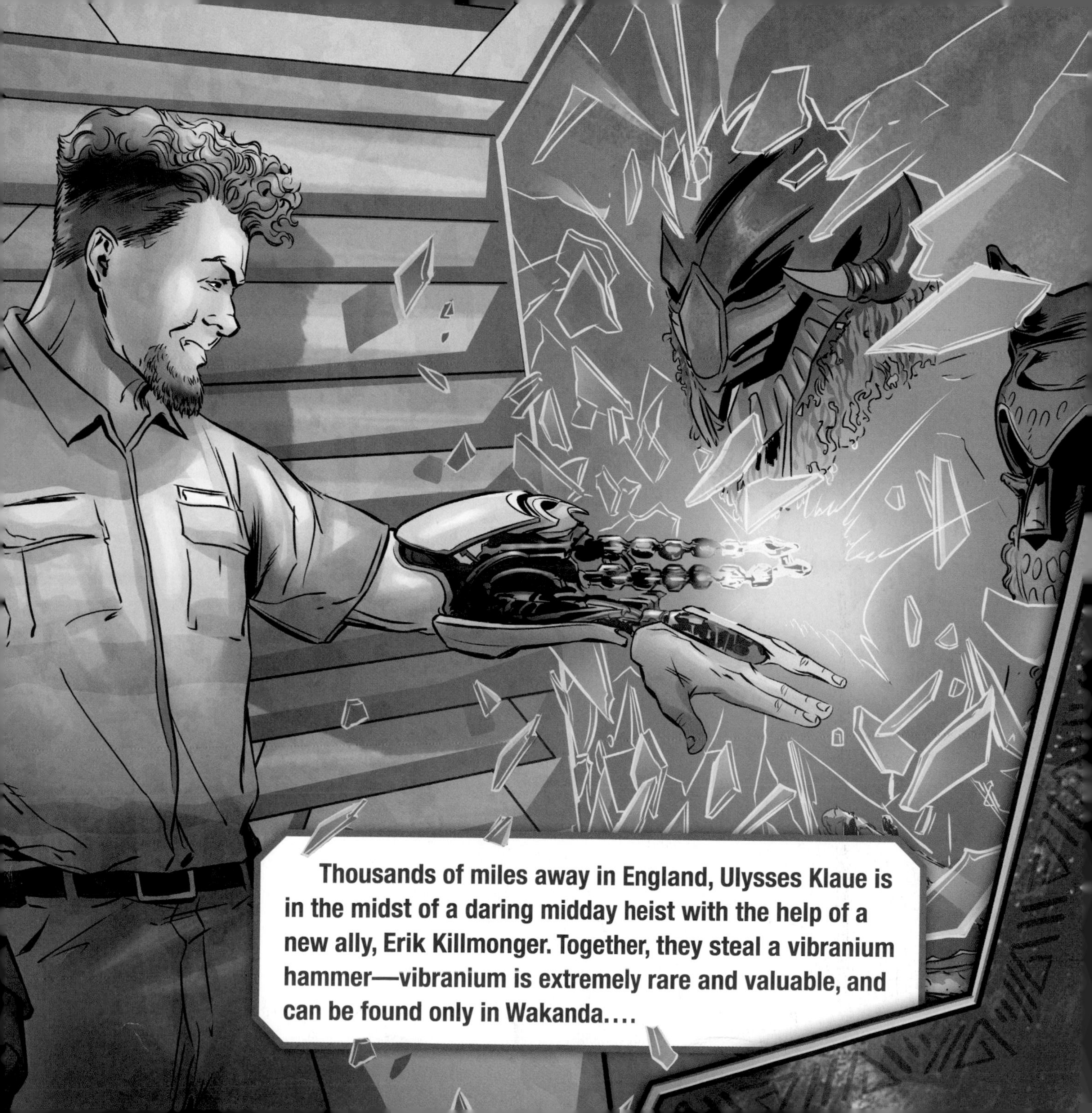

Thousands of miles away in England, Ulysses Klaue is in the midst of a daring midday heist with the help of a new ally, Erik Killmonger. Together, they steal a vibranium hammer—vibranium is extremely rare and valuable, and can be found only in Wakanda. . . .

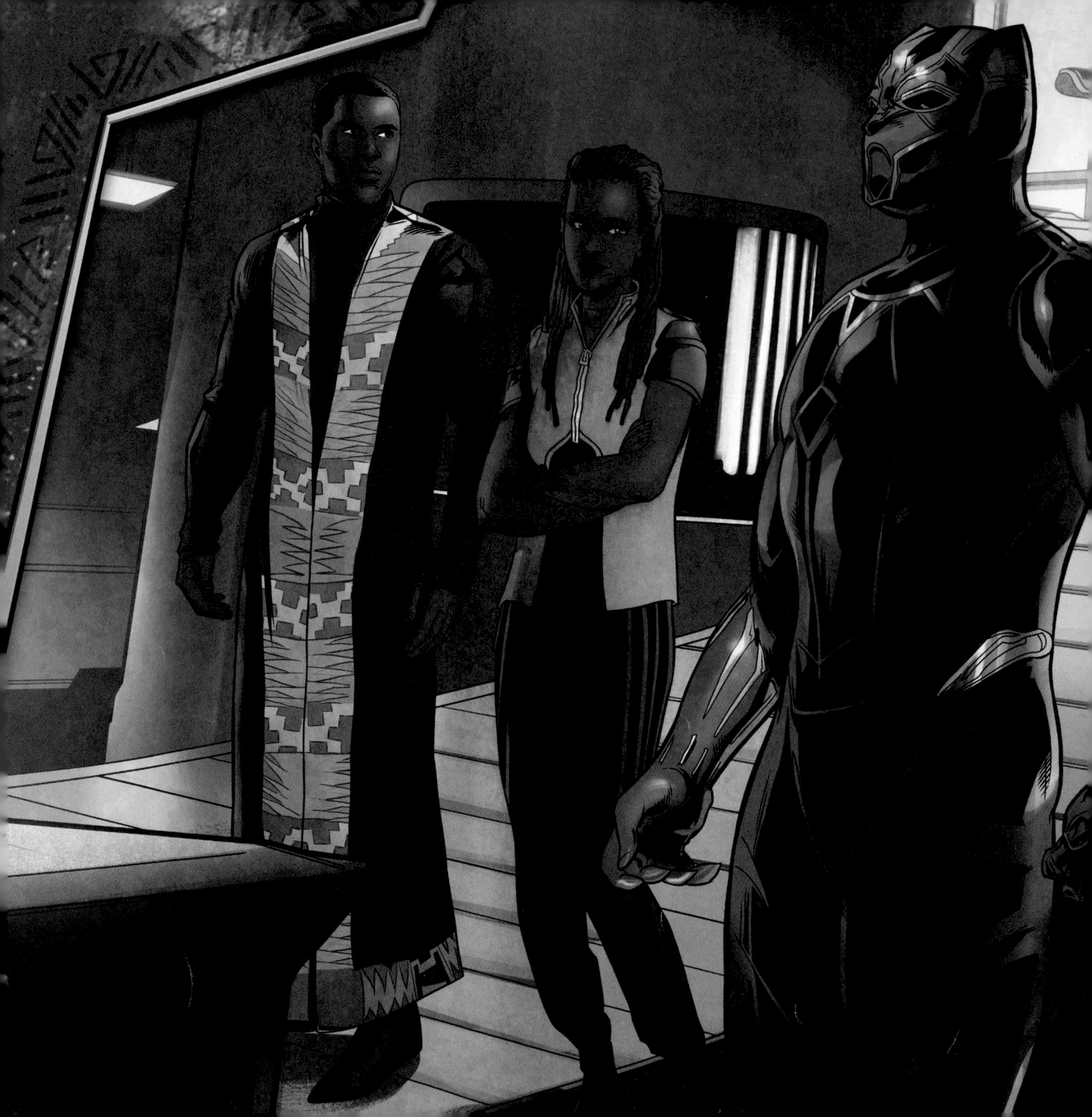

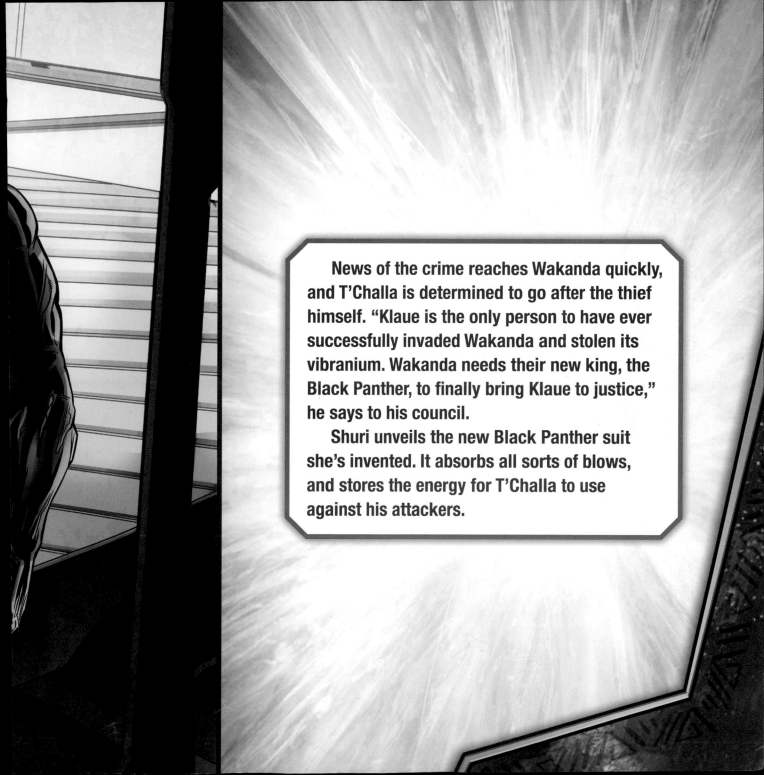

News of the crime reaches Wakanda quickly, and T'Challa is determined to go after the thief himself. "Klaue is the only person to have ever successfully invaded Wakanda and stolen its vibranium. Wakanda needs their new king, the Black Panther, to finally bring Klaue to justice," he says to his council.

Shuri unveils the new Black Panther suit she's invented. It absorbs all sorts of blows, and stores the energy for T'Challa to use against his attackers.

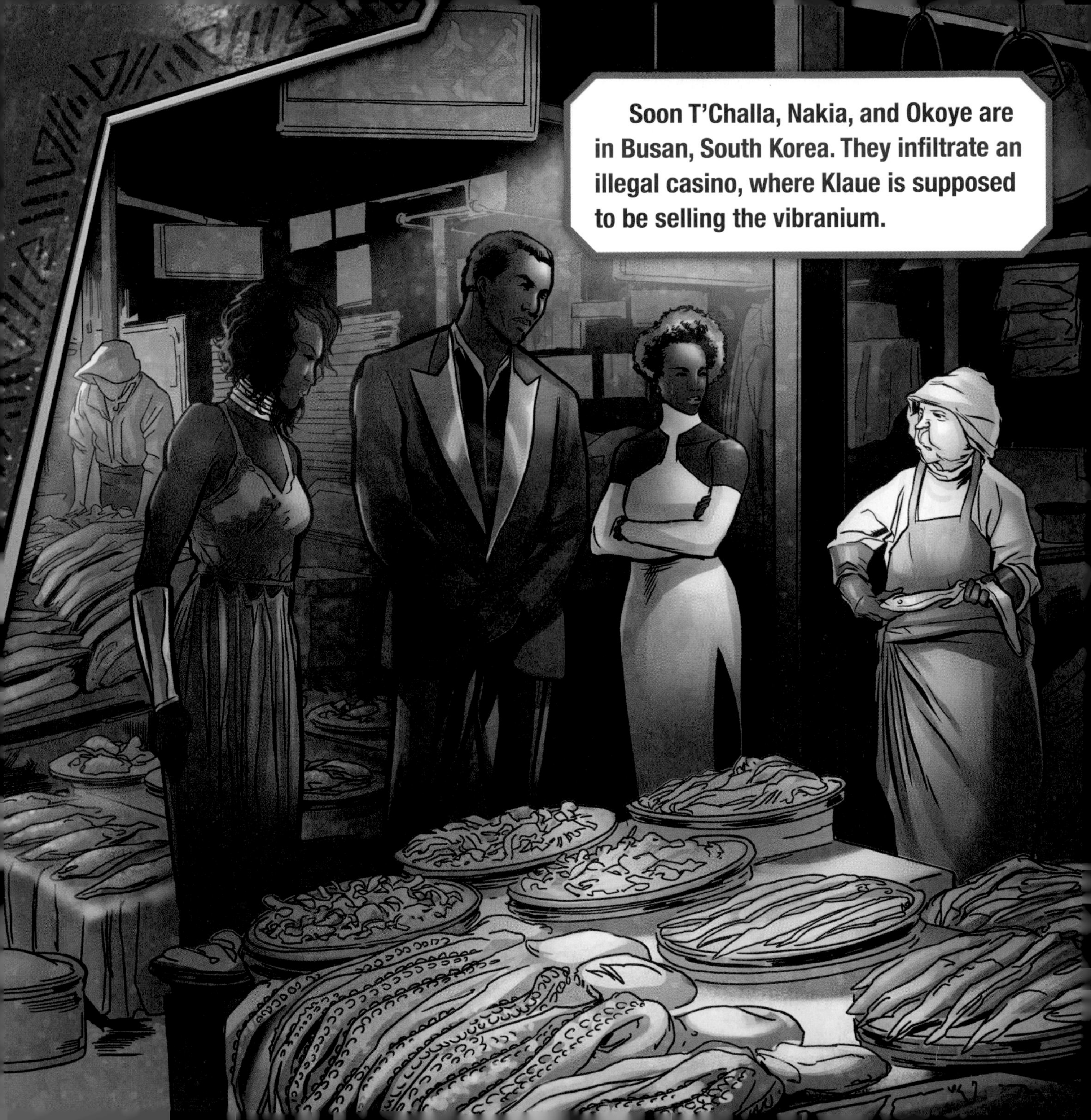
Soon T'Challa, Nakia, and Okoye are in Busan, South Korea. They infiltrate an illegal casino, where Klaue is supposed to be selling the vibranium.

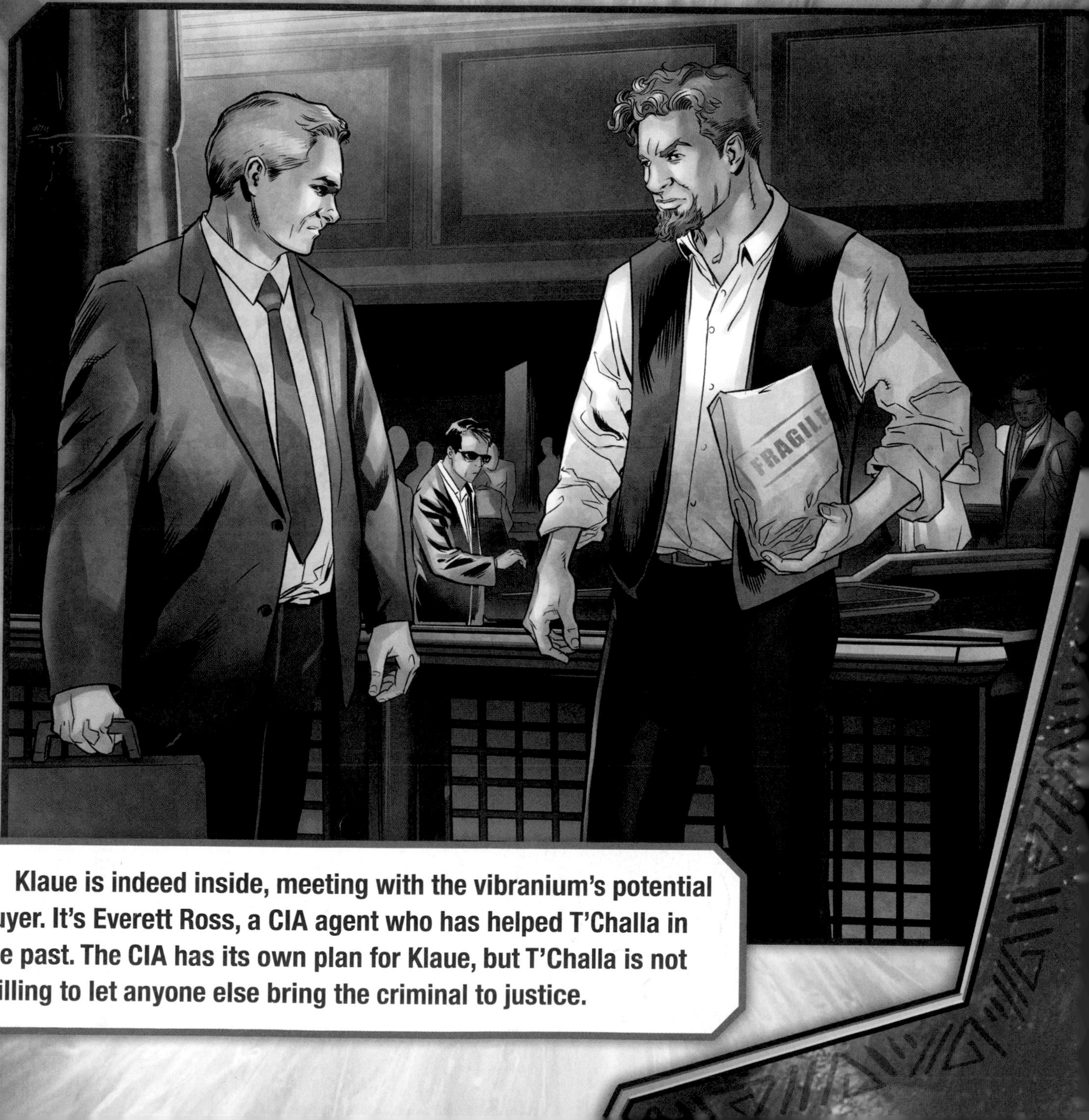
FRAGILE

Klaue is indeed inside, meeting with the vibranium's potential buyer. It's Everett Ross, a CIA agent who has helped T'Challa in the past. The CIA has its own plan for Klaue, but T'Challa is not willing to let anyone else bring the criminal to justice.

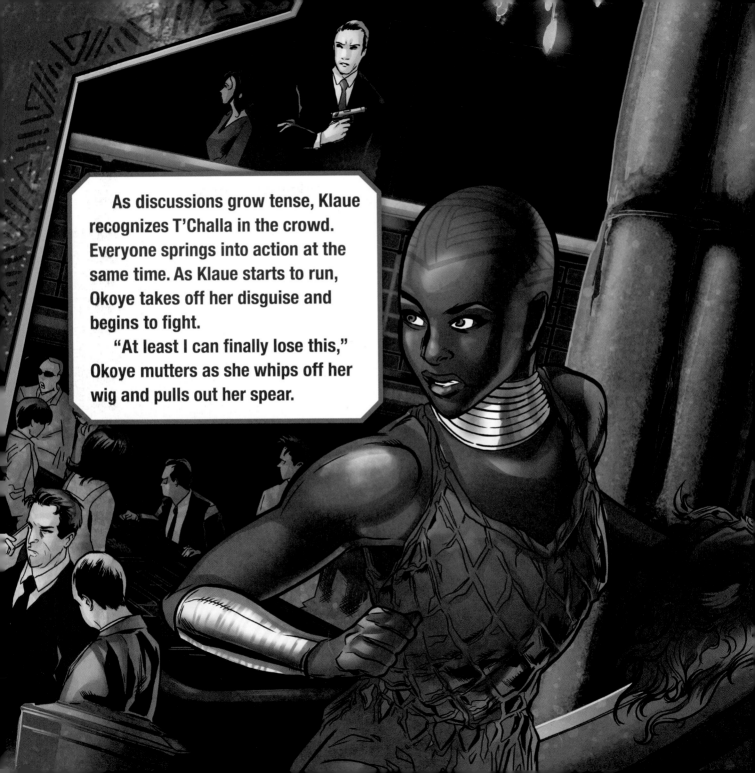

As discussions grow tense, Klaue recognizes T'Challa in the crowd. Everyone springs into action at the same time. As Klaue starts to run, Okoye takes off her disguise and begins to fight.

"At least I can finally lose this," Okoye mutters as she whips off her wig and pulls out her spear.

As T'Challa moves to grab Klaue at the exit, he's stopped by a sonic blast from Klaue's mechanical arm. Klaue has turned his hand into a high-tech weapon, and T'Challa is taken by surprise…

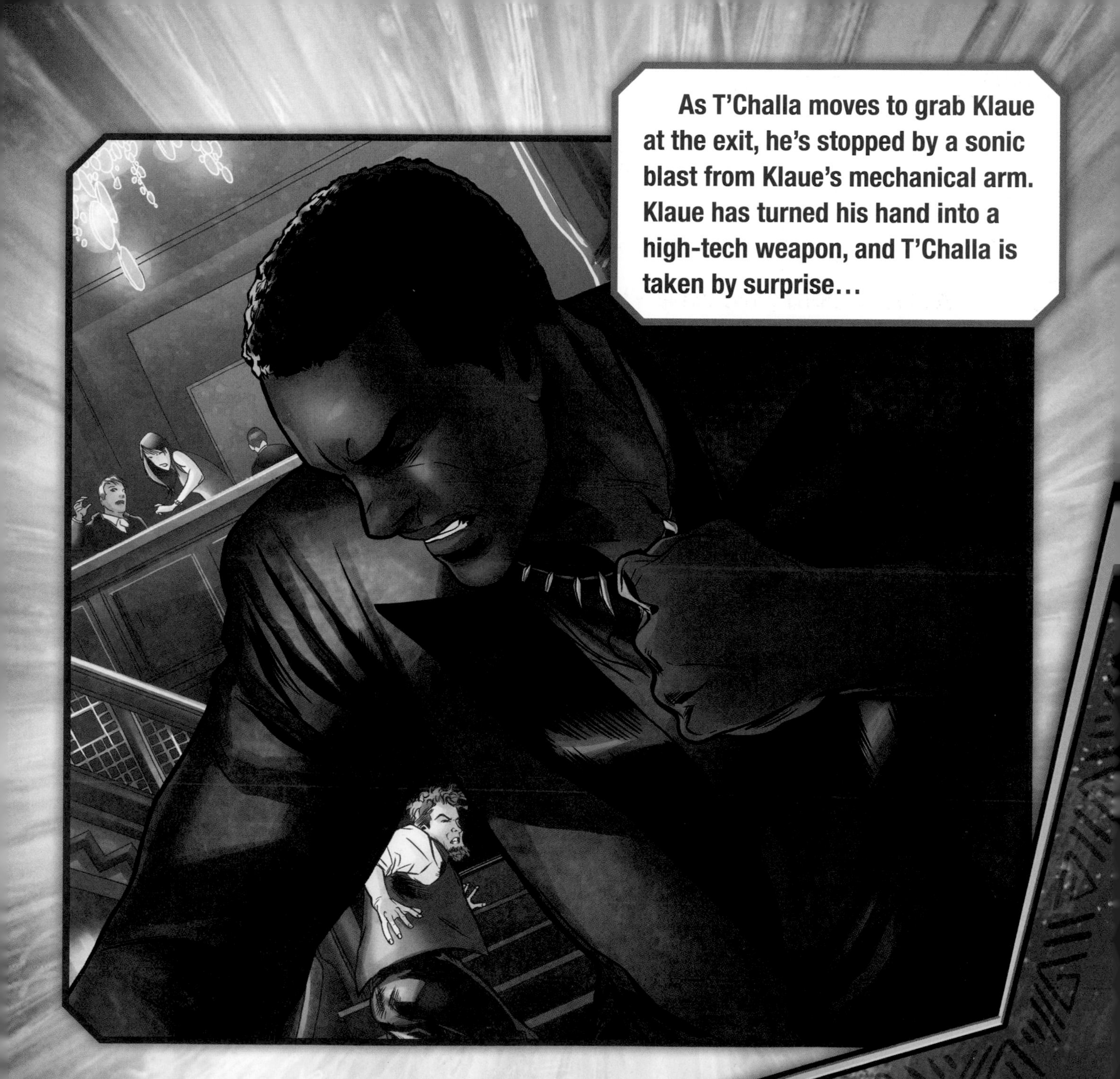

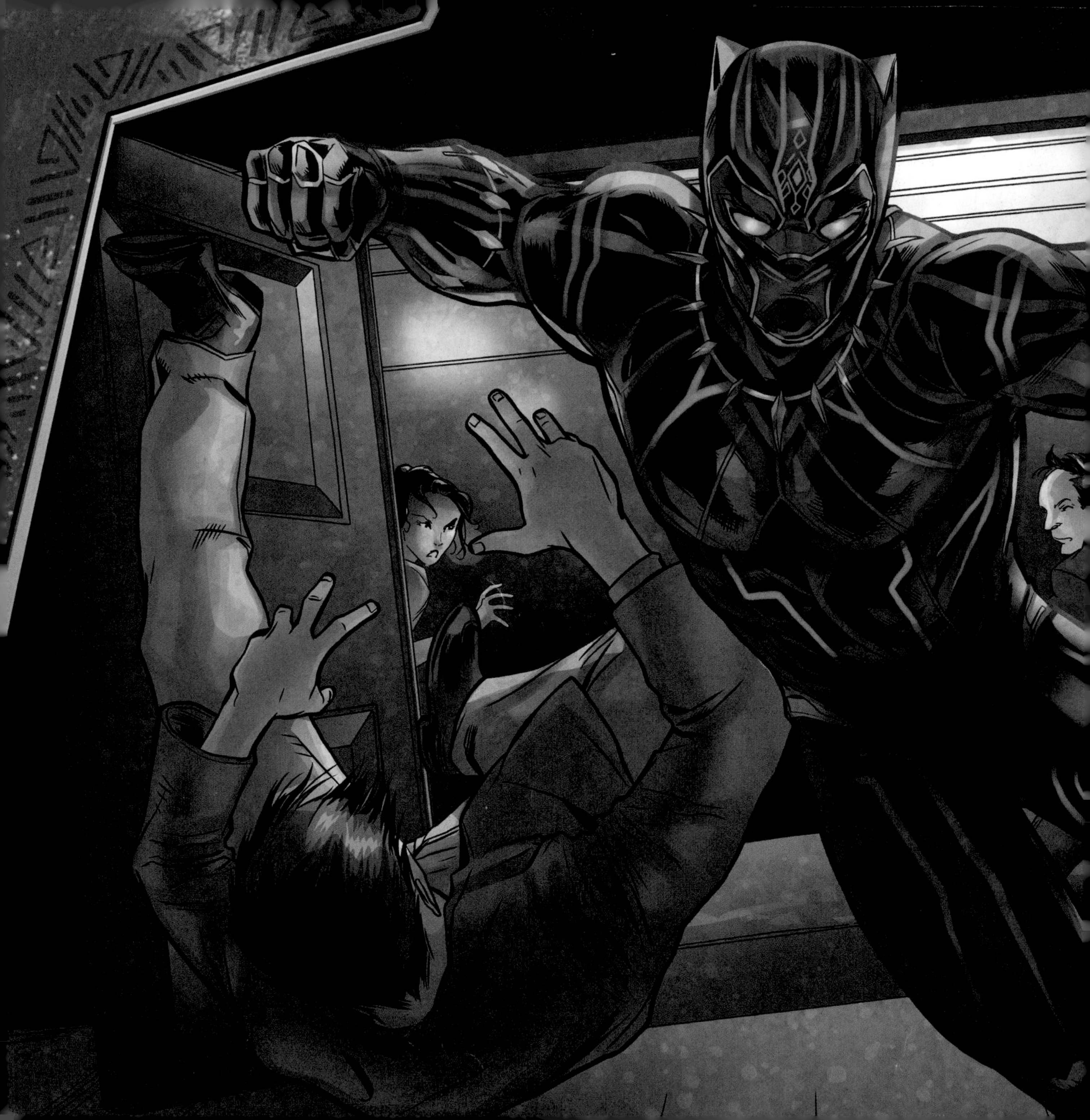

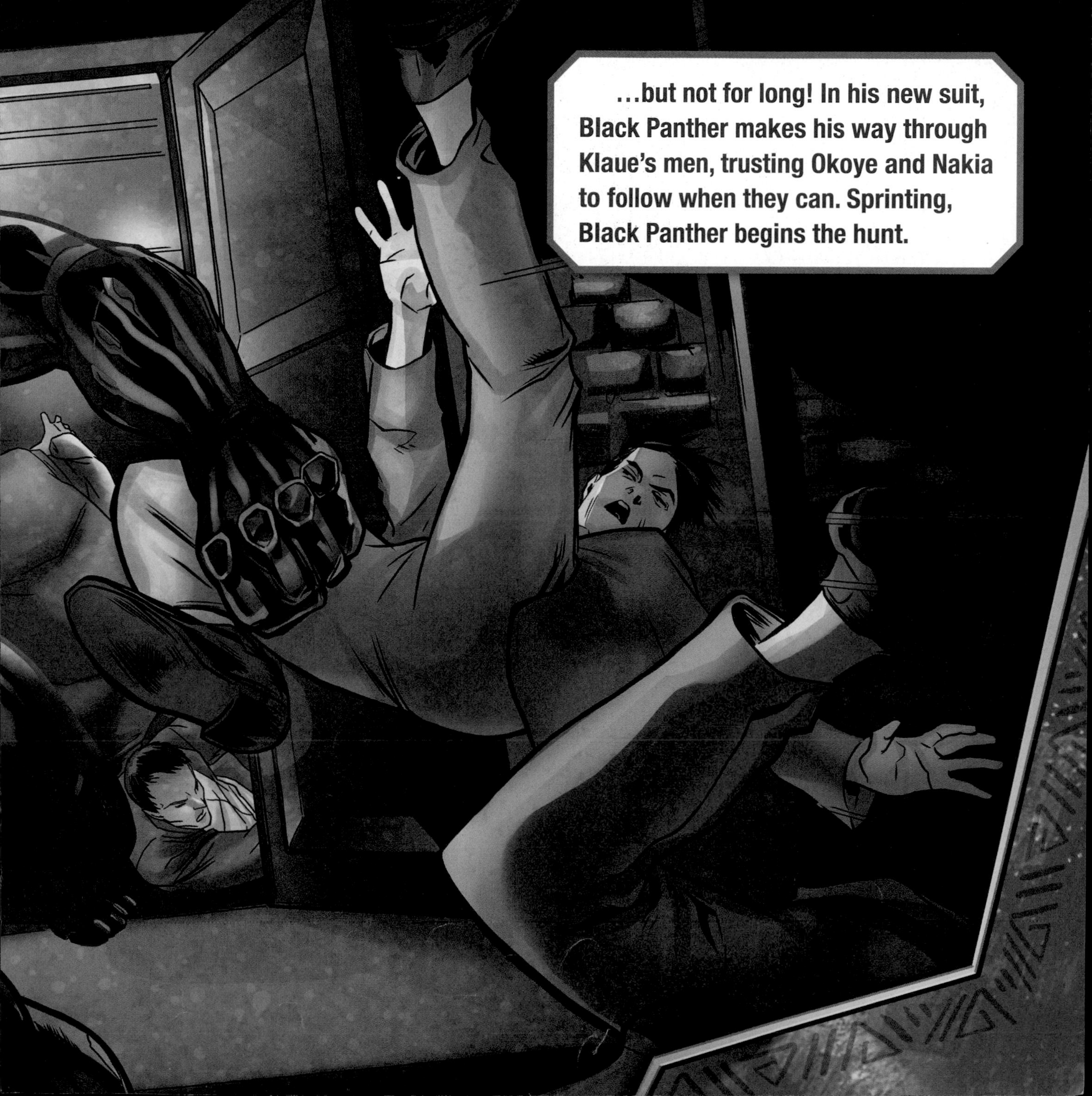
…but not for long! In his new suit, Black Panther makes his way through Klaue's men, trusting Okoye and Nakia to follow when they can. Sprinting, Black Panther begins the hunt.

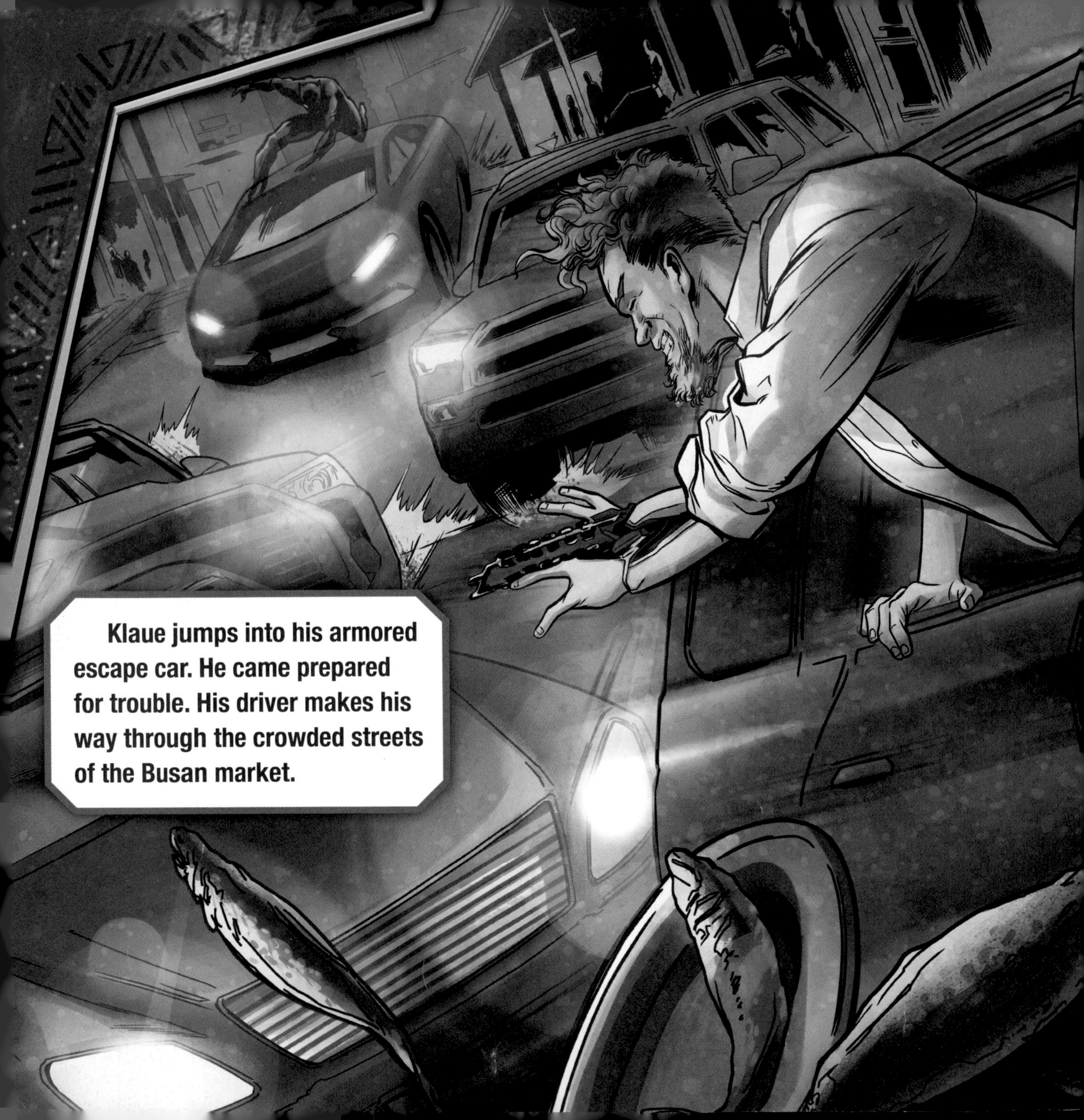
Klaue jumps into his armored escape car. He came prepared for trouble. His driver makes his way through the crowded streets of the Busan market.

Black Panther is not far behind. He uses all his skill and speed to catch up to the racing vehicle.

"Second car on your right," says Shuri through the communicator. "Hop on and let me take the wheel." The empty car starts, and the engine revs as Shuri controls it remotely. Black Panther has found his ride.

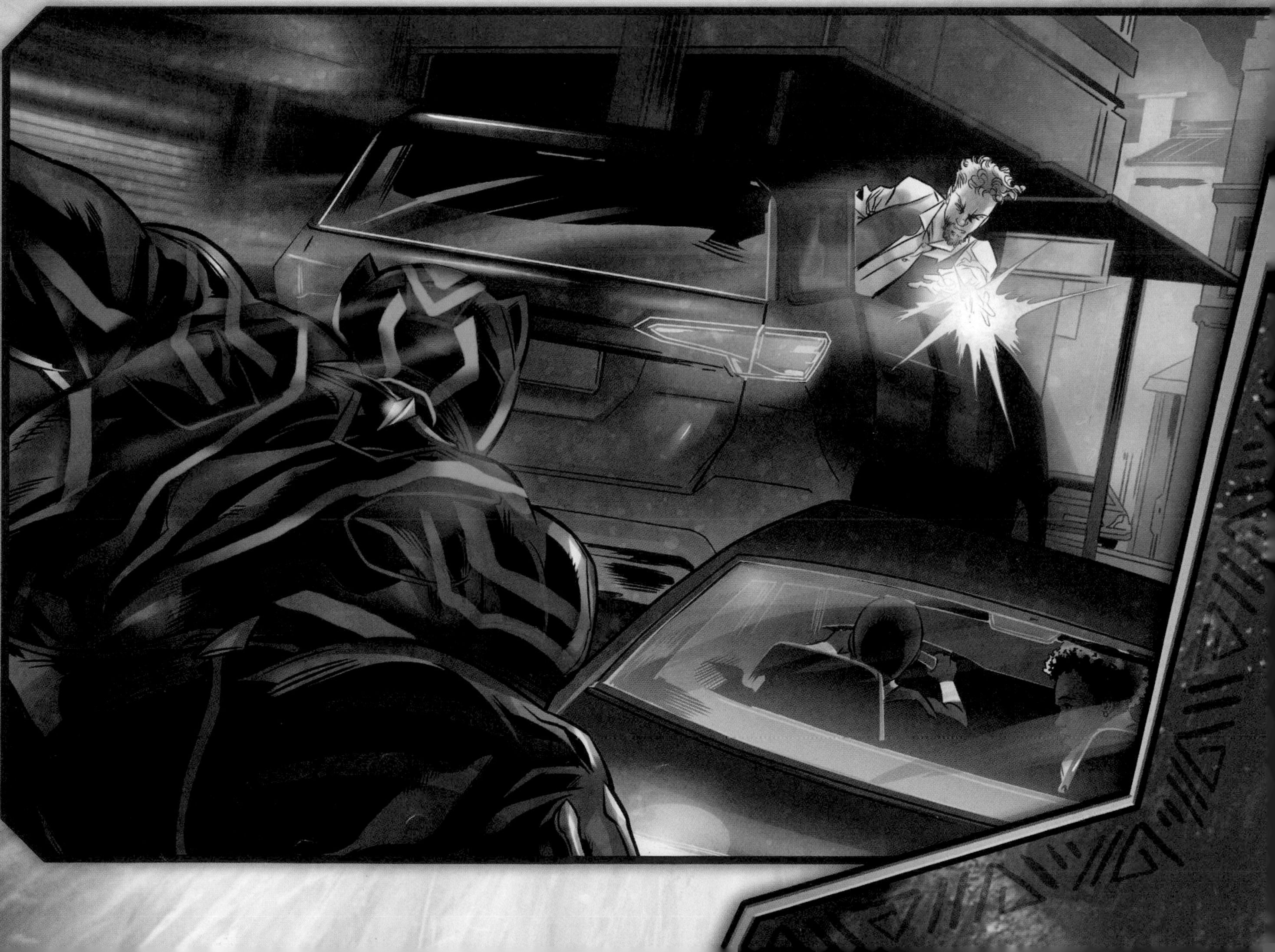

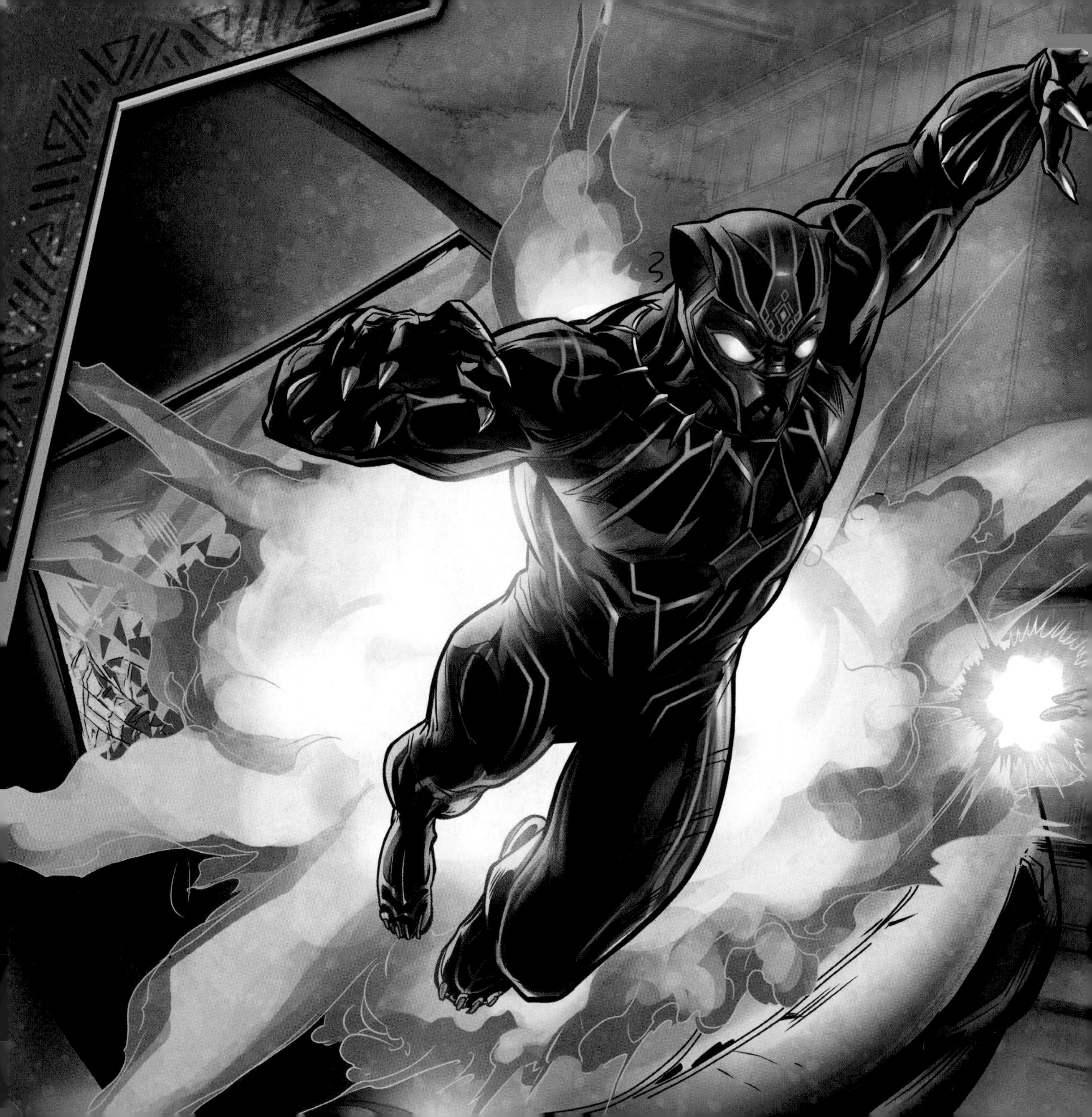

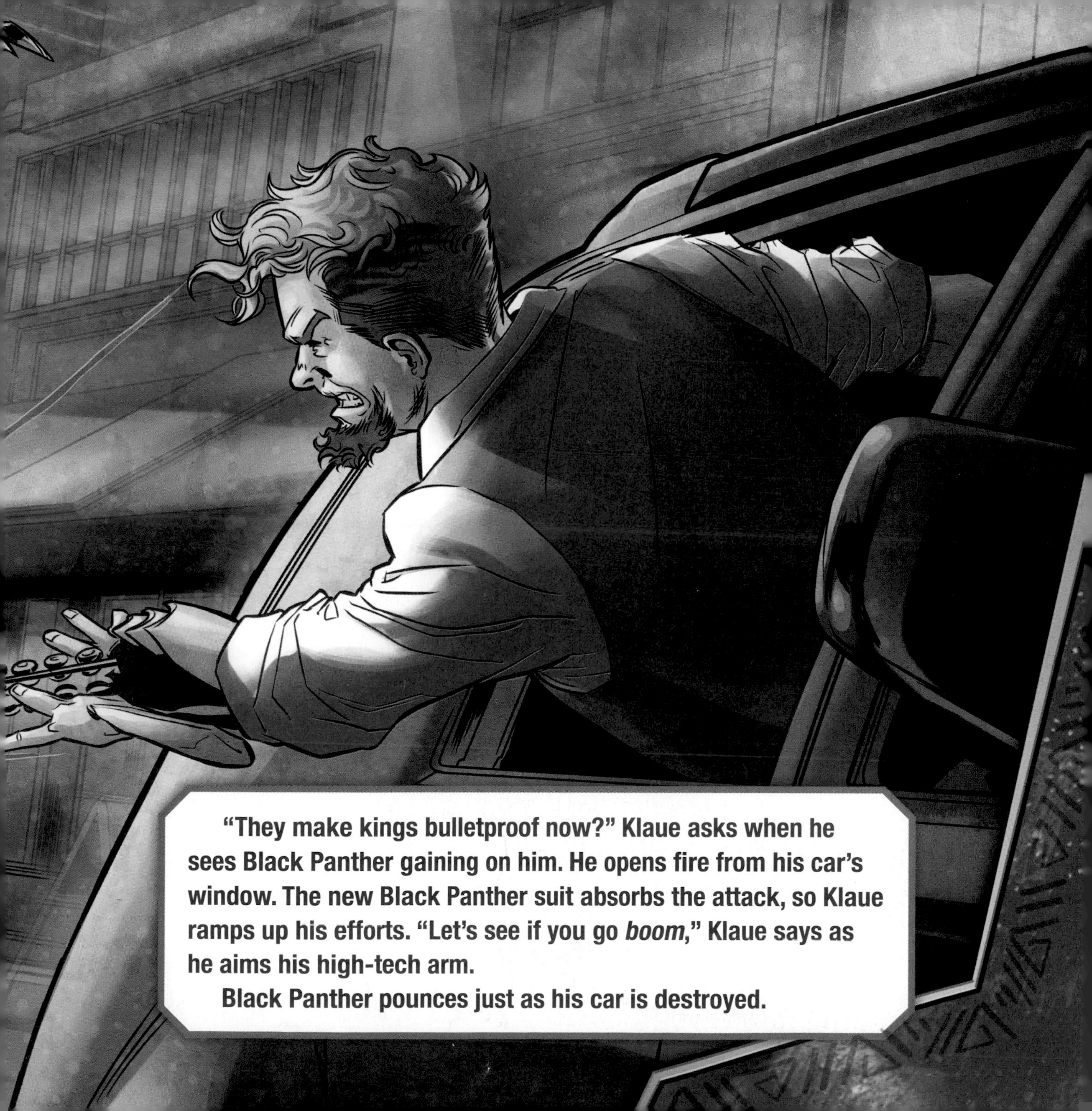

“They make kings bulletproof now?” Klaue asks when he sees Black Panther gaining on him. He opens fire from his car’s window. The new Black Panther suit absorbs the attack, so Klaue ramps up his efforts. “Let’s see if you go *boom*,” Klaue says as he aims his high-tech arm.

Black Panther pounces just as his car is destroyed.

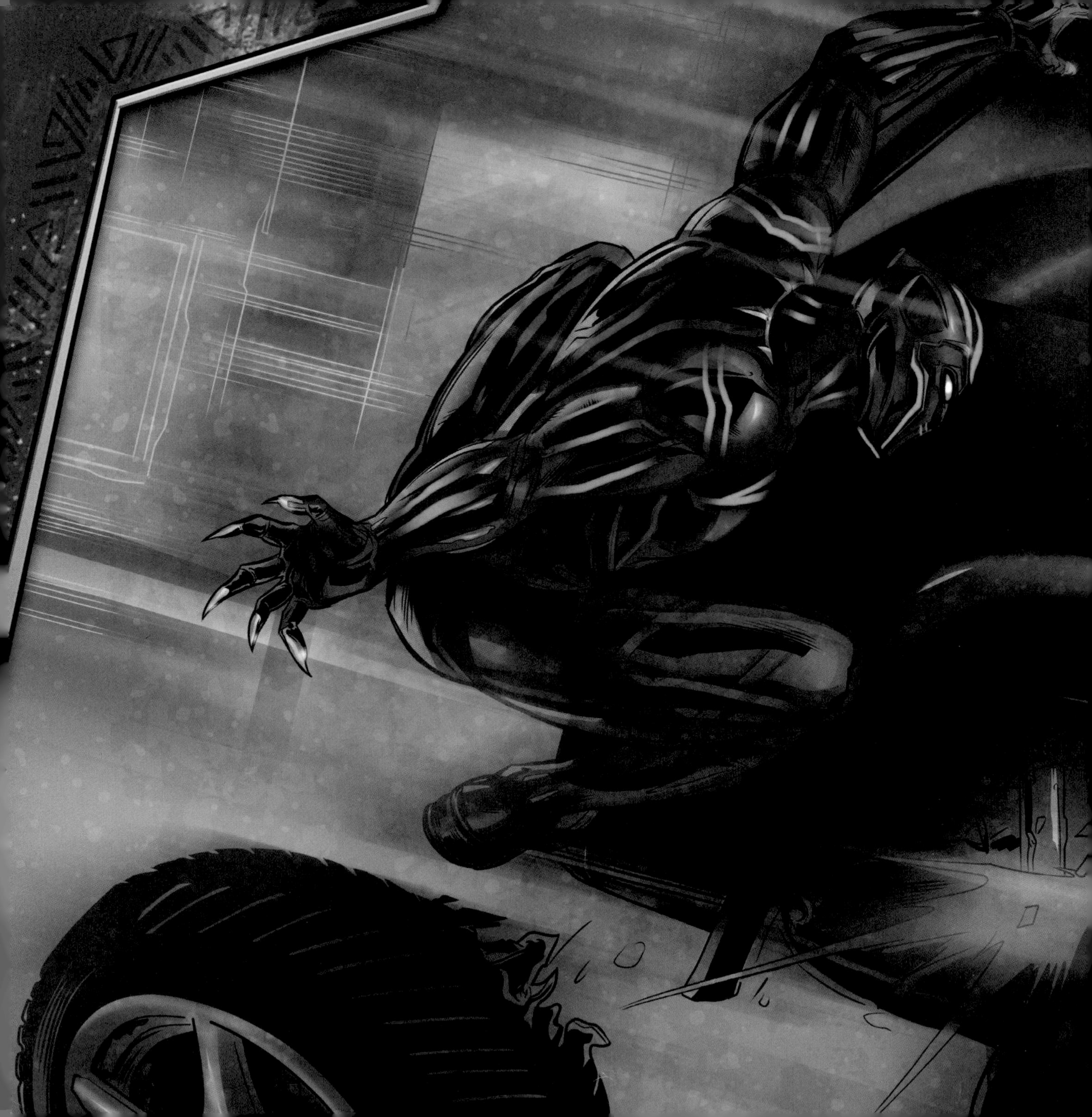

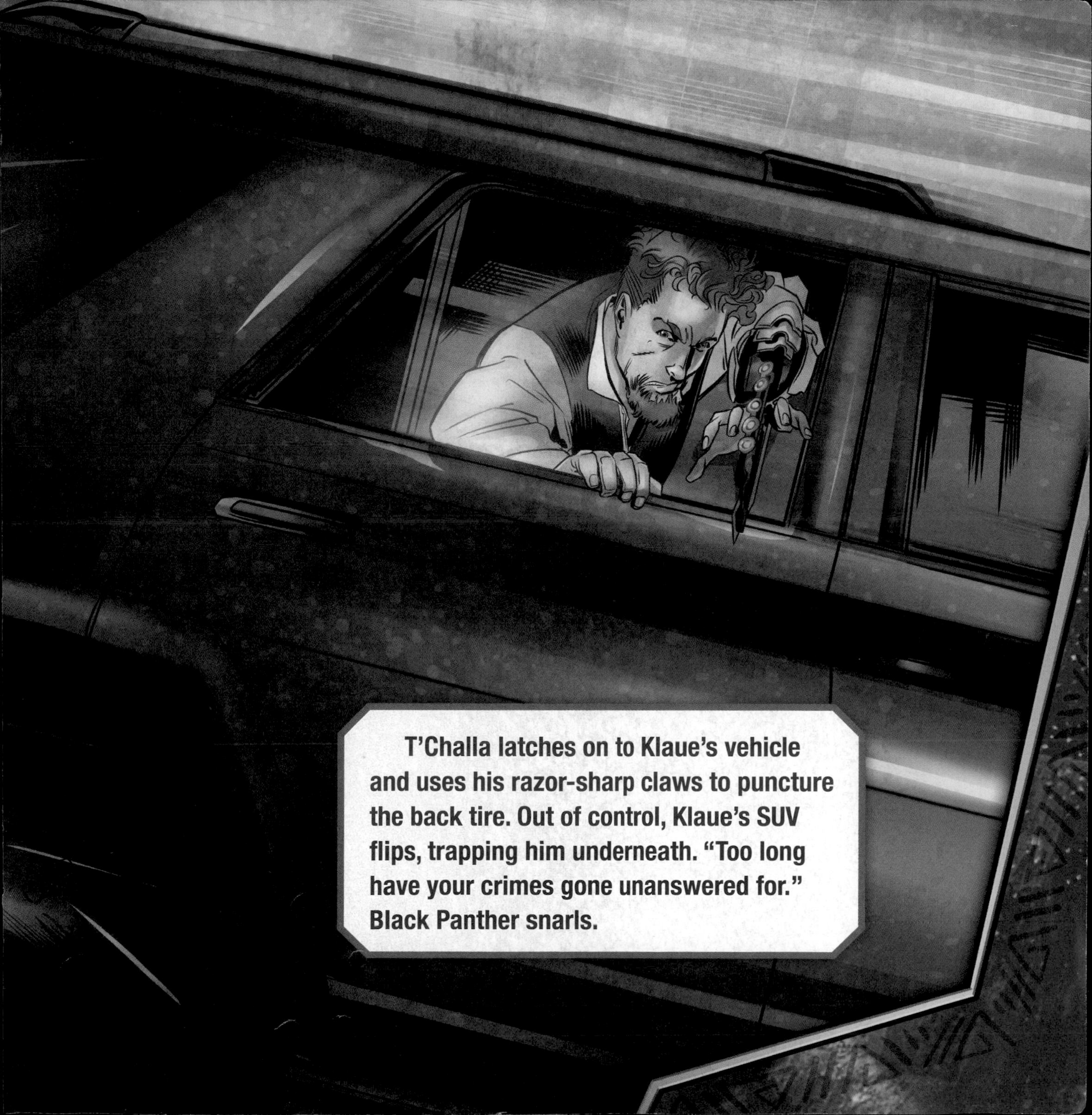

T'Challa latches on to Klaue's vehicle and uses his razor-sharp claws to puncture the back tire. Out of control, Klaue's SUV flips, trapping him underneath. "Too long have your crimes gone unanswered for." Black Panther snarls.

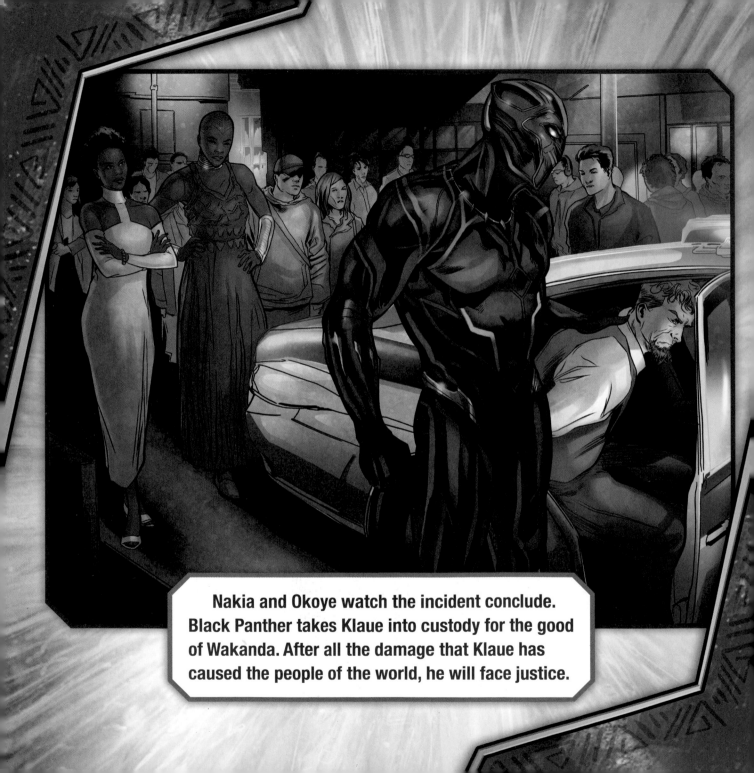

Nakia and Okoye watch the incident conclude. Black Panther takes Klaue into custody for the good of Wakanda. After all the damage that Klaue has caused the people of the world, he will face justice.

Directions: Pu
the mask, eye
string holes. Ti
each end of the
then place it on
Finally, tie the t
together in the

EL
om